The Bear and the Bird King

FROM THE BROTHERS GRIMM

RETOLD AND ILLUSTRATED BY

ROBERT BYRD

Dutton Children's Books   New York

ne fine day, the bear and the wolf went walking in the woods. The bear heard a songbird singing, so he stopped to listen.

"Tell me, Brother Wolf," he said. "What bird sings so joyfully?"

"That is the king of the birds," replied the wolf.

"Well, if he is a king," said the bear, "he must live in a fine palace. I should like to see it. Will you show me where it is?"

"That will not be so easy," said the wolf. "The king of the birds
lives high up in a tall, tall tree."

"No bother for me," said the bear. "I can climb anything."

The wolf took the bear to the Bird King's tree, and the bear
climbed up and up. But the only home he found was a simple nest
made of twigs and leaves.

The bear peeked into the nest, and there he saw six baby birds.

"Why, this doesn't look like a royal palace," he said. "And you don't look like royal children, either. You look like plain old *nasty* children to me."

The young birds were very angry.

"No, no!" they cried. "We are not nasty children. We are good children. And our father is the king of the birds!"

One baby bird flapped her wings with all her might and declared, "Bear, you will be sorry for this!"

But the bear didn't care. Laughing all the way, he climbed back down the tree and went home with the wolf.

When the king and queen of the birds returned to the nest, they found their little ones crying and upset.

"Momma, the bear was here and called us names!"

"He said we were nasty!"

"Aren't we nice children?" they cried.

"Don't you worry anymore," said the king, outraged. "Of course you are nice children. Your mother and I will take care of the bear!"

Then the king and the queen flew directly to the bear's den.

"Wake up, Old Growler," called the king.

"Why did you insult our children?" cried the queen. "You had better apologize to them or you'll be sorry!"

"Go away, you silly little birds," the bear scoffed. "Let me take my nap in peace."

"Peace!" the king shouted. "There will be no peace for you until you apologize. What do you have to say?"

But the bear only rolled over and shut his eyes, pretending to sleep.

"Then," the king declared, "this is WAR!"

And so the king of the birds declared war on the bear.

The bear was not too worried, because what harm could a silly little bird do? But just in case, as soon as he woke up, he called some

friends to help him: the lion and the ox, the deer and the elephant. The word spread, and soon every four-legged animal in the forest had agreed to help fight the Bird King.

Upon hearing this news, the king of the birds summoned to his
side all the creatures that fly through the air. Not only the birds of

every size and shape, but the gnats, the hornets, the bees, and the
flies all came to help too.

When it was time for the war to begin, the Bird King sent for the gnat.

"Gnat, you are tiny but brave," said the king. "Fly to the animals' camp and see if you can hear their secret plans."

The gnat obediently flew into the forest. He found the clearing where the animals had camped, and he hid under a leaf.

The bear was standing before the assembled group. "We must pick a leader," he said. "I would do it myself, only I would not want to take the honor from someone more deserving. Who shall it be?"

No one spoke up.

After a moment's silence, the bear made a suggestion. "Fox," he said, "you are the slyest of all. You shall be our general and lead us."

The fox was flattered, and not at all afraid. "Very well," he replied. "I shall do it. I shall be your leader. But first we will need a battle signal." The fox thought for a moment, prancing from foot to foot.

"I've got it!" he suddenly shouted. "I will use my tail. It is long and bushy and looks just like a lovely red plume. If I lift my tail straight up in the air, that means all is well. You must charge ahead, with all your might.

"But if I let my tail droop down, it means all is lost. In that case, you must run for your lives."

Now that the gnat had heard everything he needed to hear, he flew directly back to the king of the birds and gave his report.

At last the day arrived for the great battle between the creatures of the ground and the creatures of the air. All of the four-legged beasts came running and jumping and leaping with a thunderous pounding of paws. The earth trembled beneath them.

Then the king of the birds and his army came flying through the air, with such a swarming and whistling and buzzing of wings that a great wind blew. The leaves on the trees shook for miles around.

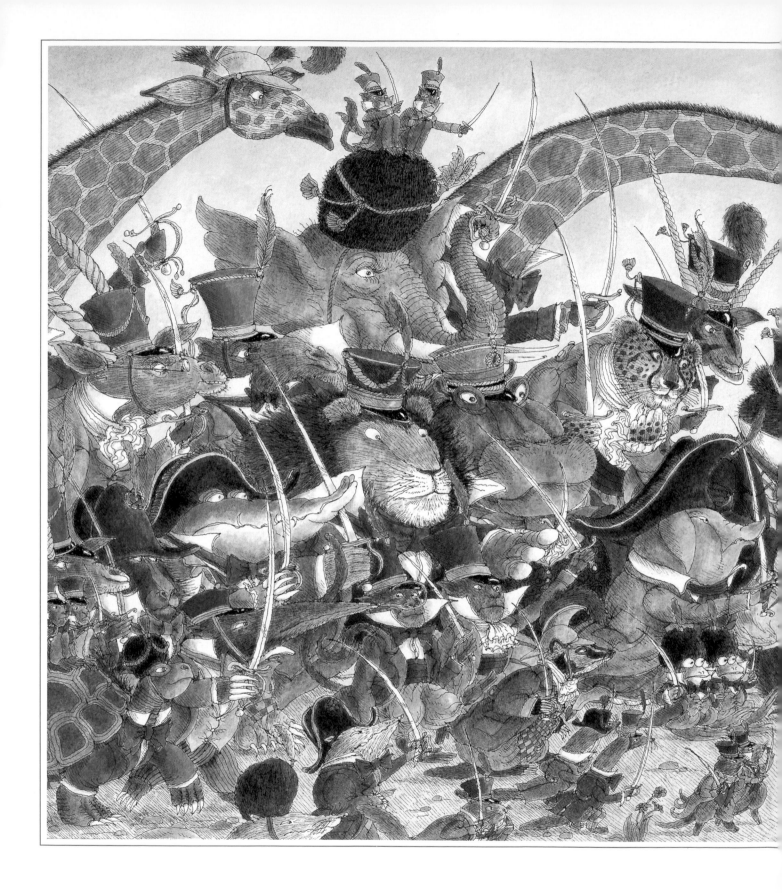

As the two armies drew face-to-face, with swords and rapiers drawn, the king of the birds whispered, "Now!" to the queen of the

bees. The tiny bee flew right under the fox's tail and stung him with
all her might.

The fox yelped with surprise and hopped up and down on one foot. But he kept his tail straight up, like a red banner in the breeze.

"Again!" whispered the Bird King. The bee readied for the charge and stung the fox a second time.

At the second sting, the fox squealed loudly and hopped up and down on both feet. But he kept his tail high in the air.

"And for the final blow!" whispered the Bird King to the bee.
After the third sting, the fox could not stand it any longer. He
let his tail droop down and bellowed loudly.

When the animals saw the signal for retreat, they thought all was lost and began to run.

They ran and they ran while the ground shook beneath their paws until, finally, all was still. The battle was over.

And the birds had won.

The king and queen flew straight home to their children.

"Rejoice!" they cried. "Eat, drink, and be merry! We have conquered the bear."

But the young birds were still upset. "Who can rejoice?" they said. "Who can eat? We cannot celebrate until the bear comes and says that we are nice children."

So the king and queen of the birds flew to the bear's den once more and called out, "Old Bear, this has gone on long enough. You must come to our nest and apologize. You must tell our babies that they are nice, good children."

But the bear would not come out. He was sulking in bed.

"Go away," he cried, and he pulled the covers over his head.

So the birds set up a great racket outside, squawking and chirping and beating their wings against the door of the den.

All of the other animals came out to see what was going on.

"Bear, come out and apologize!" someone shouted.

"You started this whole thing!"

"You had better say you are sorry!"

Finally, when the bear realized he would never get back to sleep, he put on his best clothes and crept out of his den. The other animals were quiet as he climbed up the Bird King's tree and told the young birds he was very sorry for what he had said. Then a loud cheer went up from the creatures of the ground and the creatures of the air.

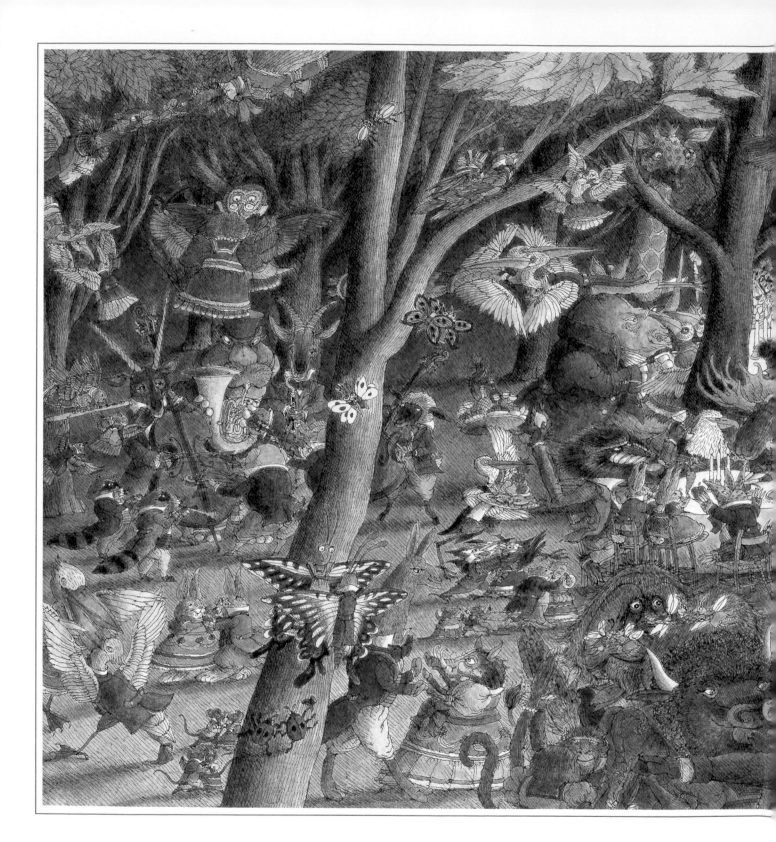

Everyone, even the bear—who did feel much better, now that he had apologized—gathered together. They had a great party and ate and drank and made merry until very late into the night.